Ahoy there, kids! Ready to sing the
SpongeBob SquarePants theme song?
I can't hear you!
OOOOOOOOOOOOOOOOOH,
Who lives in a pineapple under the sea?
SpongeBob SquarePants!
Absorbent and yellow and porous is he.
SpongeBob SquarePants!
If nautical nonsense be something you wish.
SpongeBob SquarePants!
Then drop on the deck and flop like a fish.
SpongeBob SquarePants!
SpongeBob SquarePants!
SpongeBob SquarePants!
SpongeBob SquarePants!
Sponge– Bob,   Square– Pants!
Ah ha ha ha ah har har har

Tea at the Treedome

SpongeBob stepped up to the front door of the treedome. The heavy door was made of thick steel, and it took all of SpongeBob's strength to swing it open.

Once inside, the sponge walked down a narrow hallway and faced a second door identical to the first, only this one was locked. He pressed the button of an intercom, and Sandy's voice came out of the speaker. "Hello?" she said. "Who is it?"

"Hiya, Sandy. It's me. SpongeBob."

"Hold on a sec," Sandy replied from within. "I'll empty the air lock."

Suddenly, a Klaxon horn started to honk!

"Gah!" SpongeBob cried. "What's that?"

He became even more worried when a red light began to flash!

All of a sudden, the water began to go down the drain in the floor.

Based on the TV series *SpongeBob SquarePants*®
created by Stephen Hillenburg as seen on Nickelodeon®

ISBN 0-439-34146-9

12 11 10 9 8 7 6 5   2 3 4 5 6/0

Printed in the U.S.A.

First Scholastic printing, September 2001

Tea at the Treedome

by **Terry Collins**

illustrated by **Mark O'Hare**

based on an original teleplay by

Peter Burns, Mr. Lawrence, and Paul Tibbitt

SCHOLASTIC INC.

New York   Toronto   London   Auckland   Sydney
Mexico City   New Delhi   Hong Kong   Buenos Aires

chapter one

Welcome to the sea. Beautiful, mysterious . . . and wet.

It is here where the dolphin frolics and the electric eel slithers. Where the shy octopus plays and the sea horse rides. But go farther down . . . all the way to the bottom of the ocean. Here is a world entirely different from what we know on dry land.

A strange world with different rules, funny customs . . . and unusual creatures.

"Wow! Four stingers!" a squeaky voice exclaimed as an angry jellyfish buzzed by. "Buzz away, jellyfish," the yellow box-shaped character continued in his best dramatic voice. "For soon you shall belong to . . . *SpongeBob SquarePants!*"

SpongeBob gave a few practice swings with his net in preparation to capture his prey.

Then, he readied himself as the jellyfish came around for another pass.

"Buzzzzzzzzzz," said the jellyfish.

SpongeBob buzzed back in his best jellyfish impersonation to lure him into his trap. "Steady," he whispered, readying his net. "Steady . . ."

The jellyfish slowed down and hovered over a blue sea anemone.

"Yes!" SpongeBob screeched, bounding out of hiding and bringing down his net.

The jellyfish avoided the attack and swam to the left.

SpongeBob followed suit, swinging the net in a

sideways arc . . . but somehow caught himself instead!

Hanging in his own net, SpongeBob watched sadly as the jellyfish zipped home to Jellyfish Fields.

Disappointed, SpongeBob continued to look for other jellyfish, but none were to be found. However, he did notice a funny-looking creature in a space suit wrestling a giant clam. . . .

SpongeBob did a double take. Space suit!? Could it be . . . space aliens?

He wiggled out of his net and ran toward the scene.

Upon closer inspection, SpongeBob saw that the space suit was actually a white high-tech diving suit. As for the clam . . . well, it was huge! And mean!

The spry fighter growled like a grizzly bear and used a combination of judo and karate—plus some moves SpongeBob had never even seen

before—to fight the threatening clam.

The creature in a space helmet gave a final cry of triumph and conked the gray shell of the giant clam. It was this move that allowed SpongeBob to clearly see the fighter's face for the first time.

Where have I seen this before? SpongeBob wondered. Reaching into his pocket, he took out his handy *Barks Junior Field Guide*.

SpongeBob frantically flipped through the pages. "Ah-ha!" he cried, finding a page with a picture of the being in the diving suit. However, in the field guide, a furry head was exposed.

"Land squirrel," SpongeBob read aloud. "She's a land squirrel . . . whatever *that* is."

Suddenly, the squirrel gave out a loud grunt of surprise as the clam bit her leg.

"That little squirrel is in trouble!" SpongeBob announced. "This looks like a job for . . . SpongeBob!"

chapter two

SpongeBob hiked up his square pants and raced to the land squirrel's rescue.

As he ran down the hill, he saw the squirrel jerk her leg free.

Gaining the upper paw, she began battering the clam like a loose penny in a supercharged washing machine!

"Take that! And this! And a mouth of that!" the squirrel cried in a strong Texas accent as she socked and stomped.

The clam rocked back and forth, weakening from the attack.

SpongeBob was fascinated. He'd never seen *anyone* like this squirrel person.

"Y'all need to learn some manners!" the squirrel snorted as she picked up her enemy and held it above her head.

SpongeBob closed his eyes in fear. The clam was ten times bigger than the little land squirrel! If she dropped it, she'd be squished like a bug!

SpongeBob opened his eyes just in time to see the feisty squirrel body slam the battered clam into the sand face first!

"There!" she said. "Mean ol' clam. You know, you're 'bout as ugly as homemade soup!"

"Hooray, land squirrel!" SpongeBob cheered. He was amazed at what he had seen. He *had* to befriend this brave warrior!

Just then, SpongeBob saw the giant clam wiggle like a worm on a hook, trying to pull itself from the silt and muck on the ocean floor.

"Look out!" SpongeBob yelled. But his warning was too late!

The monster clam was free and was heading for the land squirrel!

The clam soared through the air . . . and tumbled toward the unsuspecting squirrel! She never knew what hit her as the clam's maw snapped shut like a bear trap, trapping her inside!

"Hold on, little squirrel!" SpongeBob yelled, his scrawny legs a blur as he raced to his new companion's rescue.

To fight this foe, SpongeBob would need to call on the discipline of . . . karate.

He struck a pose, one skinny arm crooked into the shape of a striking cobra.

"Yah! Ha! Hweee!" he shouted, using the battle cries of a karate master.

"You have fought well, giant clam," said

SpongeBob, honoring his opponent. "Prepare to be vanquished!"

First he hopped onto his oversized enemy. Then, reaching down with both hands, SpongeBob gripped the stiff upper lip of the oversized clam and pulled with all of his might.

SpongeBob gritted his teeth and gave a final Herculean effort—an effort so great, the snap of his square pants popped off!

"HYNUHH!" SpongeBob grunted. "HYNUHH!"

And then, the mouth of the mammoth clam began to inch open with a creaking sound. SpongeBob was so amazed, he nearly let go. "Hey!" he said in disbelief. "I'm actually doing it."

What SpongeBob could not see was the land squirrel pushing the clam's giant jaws open from inside.

"YA!" the squirrel snarled from behind the glass of her helmet as she struggled to free herself. "Yah! Yah! Yah!"

As the clam bucked like an angry bull, SpongeBob was tossed into the air. The squirrel hopped out of the clam's mouth and landed on her feet, ready for more action.

But, before she could make a move, SpongeBob reentered the fray. "Your shell is mine!" he said determinedly as he grabbed the giant's muscular tongue.

The squirrel gaped in surprise, right before the clam's mouth slammed shut, trapping the heroic SpongeBob inside!

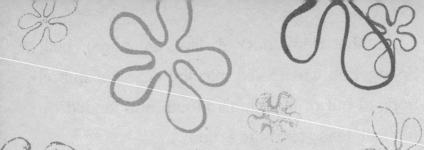

chapter three

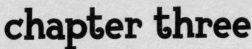

"Hold on there, little square dude!" the squirrel cried. "I'm a'comin'!"

She flipped the clam up like she was tossing a coin. When it landed, the fighting squirrel then moved on to some of her expert karate moves.

"Yah!" she cried, unleashing a karate chop!

"Hah!" she added, uncoiling a karate kick!

"Yah-hah!" she finished, unspooling a series of master moves, making the clam spin like a top.

The clam's mouth fell open, and a dazed and

confused SpongeBob staggered out.

"Wha' happened?" SpongeBob asked, dizzy from his wild ride inside the mollusk.

The squirrel stomped on the edge of the clam's lip with her boot, and it stood up on one end. She then proceeded to spin the shelled creature like a top, punching and jabbing at a rapid pace before delivering a final uppercut that sent the clam sailing up, up, and far away toward the forbidden lands of Jellyfish Fields!

"Howdy!" the squirrel said, looking down at SpongeBob.

"Hey!" SpongeBob said brightly. "You like karate too!"

The squirrel obliged by assuming the pose of the swooping crane.

"Awesome! So, what's your name?" SpongeBob asked.

"Sandy," she said. "Sandy Cheeks."

Sandy leaped up and went through a series of

karate fighting stances. "What do y'all call yourself?" she asked as she moved across the ocean floor.

SpongeBob grinned and ran toward a curved wall. "I'm . . . SpongeBo-o-o-o-o-o-ob!" he yelled as he ran up the wall, executed a perfect backflip, and landed at a forty-five-degree angle on the corner of his head directly in front of Sandy.

"Well, SpongeBob, take a gander at this!" Sandy announced, leaping over to a rock the size of SpongeBob's pineapple home in Bikini Bottom.

Closing her eyes, Sandy summoned up all of her inner strength and, without a sound, gave the massive boulder a single karate chop.

All was still.

Then, the rock began to vibrate, sending ripples through the water.

The rock continued to shake, finally exploding into a million tiny pieces that scattered in all directions.

A stray pebble bounced off SpongeBob's forehead. "Ooh," he said, dumbfounded at the little squirrel's amazing display of karate.

Snapping out of his trance, SpongeBob tried to act unimpressed. "Oh, yeah?" he said nonchalantly. "Watch this!"

SpongeBob raised his arms, and then, faster than the eye could follow, stuck his right hand into the groove of his left armpit. "Observe," he said.

Then, he pumped his left arm up and down. BRAAAAP! BRAAAAP! BRAAAAP!

Sandy fell back on her tail with an uncontrollable case of the giggles.

After regaining her composure, she gave SpongeBob a playful chop on the top of his square head. "I like you, SpongeBob. We could be tighter than bark on a tree!"

SpongeBob leaped up, copying Sandy's karate move and chopping her on the glass helmet she wore. "I like you, too, Sandy. Hai-YAH!"

BONK!

"Yeow!" SpongeBob cried, his tiny yellow hand aching from the mock blow. "What is that thing on your head, anyway?"

"Why, that's my air helmet," Sandy replied, knocking the thick glass with her knuckles.

"Neat!" SpongeBob said. "May I try it on?"

Sandy laughed. "Heck, no!" she said. "I need it to breathe. I gotta have my air."

Not wanting to be left out of a good thing, SpongeBob announced, "Me too. I love air! Air is good!"

The squirrel looked at SpongeBob in shock. "No kiddin'?" she asked.

SpongeBob flashed Sandy his most confident grin. "No kiddin'!" he said.

Truth be told, SpongeBob wasn't sure what this "air" was.

But if his new friend liked it so much, why, he was sure air had to be a most excellent thing!

chapter four

"Yup, air's my middle name!" SpongeBob said, sticking his hands in his pockets and rocking on his heels. "The more air the better! Can't get enough of that air!"

Sandy clapped her paws together with delight. "Shee-oot! That's great!"

SpongeBob blushed and smiled. He was starting to love this air stuff!

Sandy reached into a pouch of her diving suit and took out a sheet of paper and a pencil.

Scribbling quickly, she handed SpongeBob a freshly drawn map to her place.

"How about coming over this afternoon to my treedome for tea and cookies, then?" she said. "How does three o'clock sound?"

"Super!" SpongeBob said. He was so excited, his body slowly started to float, allowing his feet to levitate above the ocean floor.

"Well, I gotta mosey on back," Sandy said, turning to go. "Now, don't be late!"

"Okay! See ya later!" SpongeBob said, waving good-bye. He continued to float, watching and waiting until Sandy disappeared.

Then, panic struck!

"Patrick! Patrick! Patrick!" SpongeBob yelled as he raced home. Turning around the corner, he jogged past his own orange pineapple home, past the Tiki-head lair of his neighbor Squidward, and approached a large rock at the other end of the street.

"Patrick!" SpongeBob called. "Patrick!"

Taking a nap on top of the rock was a pudgy pink starfish in blue Hawaiian shorts.

This was Patrick Star, SpongeBob's best friend.

"Patrick, wake up!" SpongeBob called as he bounced with glee. "What's air?"

Patrick lifted up his green sunglasses and peered down at SpongeBob. "Huh?" he said with a yawn. "What's going on?"

SpongeBob stood tall and announced, "Well, I just met this girl, and she invited me to a tea party, and—"

"Way to go, SpongeBob!" the starfish interrupted, giving his buddy a hearty thumbs-up.

SpongeBob returned the thumbs-up. "Thanks. But, get this . . . she wears a hat full of air."

"A hat full of *hair?*" Patrick asked.

"No, air! Air!" SpongeBob corrected.

Patrick's wide smile turned into a look of confusion. He puzzled over SpongeBob's statement for a moment, and finally asked, "Do you mean she puts on airs?"

SpongeBob shrugged his skinny shoulders. "I guess so," he said.

Patrick slid down the rock and stood in front of his pal. "No problem," he said. "Puttin' on airs is just fancy talk. If you wanna be fancy, I can help."

"Really?" SpongeBob said.

"Sure," Patrick replied, holding up one arm and sticking his little finger out. "Now, if you want to impress her, just hold your pinkie like this. The higher you hold it, the fancier you are."

SpongeBob lifted a crooked pinkie. "How's that?" he asked.

"Higher!" Patrick commanded, thrusting his own pinkie into the sky.

SpongeBob followed suit, sticking his pinkie up as far as his spindly arm would stretch. "Like that?" he asked in a pained voice.

Patrick nodded. "Now, that's fancy! They

should call you *SpongeBob FancyPants!*"

SpongeBob took out the map to Sandy's house and held it high above his head, pinkie extended. "Ready, coach!"

Patrick rubbed his chin. "Something's missing," he said. Looking over at Squidward's house, the hefty starfish spotted what he was seeking. "Wait a sec," he said, bounding across his neighbor's front yard.

Squidward popped his head out of his second-story window. "Stay off my lawn, you blob!" he yelled in a whiny voice. "That goes for you, too, SpongeBob!"

"Hi, Squidward!" SpongeBob replied. "I'm going to a tea party!"

"Like I care," Squidward retorted, and slammed his window shut.

Patrick jogged back over and handed a bouquet of bubble-tip sea flowers to SpongeBob. "I borrowed these from Squidward's garden," he

30

said. "Can't go to a girl's house without flowers!"

SpongeBob slapped his square forehead with his hand. "Duh! I should've known that!"

Patrick winked. "That's what you've got me for!"

As the two buddies left Bikini Bottom and made their way toward Sandy's treedome, Patrick continued to lecture on the finer points of going to a tea party.

"Good manners are important, SpongeBob," the starfish said. "You should say yes and no and thank you and please, and never, *ever,* ask for anything unless your host offers it to you first."

"Yes. No. Thank you. Please. Don't ask. Got it," SpongeBob replied.

Sandy's map was easy to read, and soon enough they were outside her bubble-shaped home.

Patrick took up position outside the protective dome and gave SpongeBob a final pep talk. "Remember," he said. "When in doubt, pinkie out. You can do it, SpongeBob! I'll be watchin'."

chapter five

SpongeBob stepped up to the front door of the treedome. The heavy door was made of thick steel, and it took all of SpongeBob's strength to swing it open.

Once inside, the sponge walked down a narrow hallway and faced a second door identical to the first, only this one was locked. He pressed the button of an intercom, and Sandy's voice came out of the speaker. "Hello?" she said. "Who is it?"

"Hiya, Sandy. It's me. SpongeBob."

"Hold on a sec," Sandy replied from within. "I'll empty the air lock."

Suddenly, a Klaxon horn started to honk!

"Gah!" SpongeBob cried. "What's that?"

He became even more worried when a red light began to flash!

All of a sudden, the water began to go down the drain in the floor. SpongeBob struggled with the door, but it wouldn't open. He began to wheeze. The flowers from Squidward's yard sagged in SpongeBob's hand. His body started to sag as well. SpongeBob felt . . . lightheaded. His eyes bulged in their sockets as he started to cough.

"Sandy! Sandy! Open up!" he screamed. "Open the door, Sandy!"

The land squirrel swung open the steel door to her home. "What's the rush?" she asked.

SpongeBob didn't answer as he fell to the ground on his face, flopping around like a goldfish out of its bowl.

Flipping over onto his back, SpongeBob looked up at Sandy. "Something's gone terribly wrong!" he gasped. "There's no water in here!"

Sandy helped SpongeBob to his feet. "'Course there's no water, silly. Nothin' in here but air!"

Even as he felt his brain beginning to dry out, SpongeBob tried to focus on what Sandy was saying. "No . . . water?" he wheezed.

"Nope! Just good, clean Texas air!" Sandy said. "That ain't a problem, is it?"

SpongeBob gave the squirrel a ghastly grin as his brittle lips peeled back from his teeth. "Problem? Ha-ha! Nope, nothing wrong here!"

"Yee-haw!" Sandy cried, chopping the air as she practiced her karate. "That's what I like to hear! We can work on our moves together!"

SpongeBob, his face still trapped in the awful smile, nodded in agreement. He wasn't sure what Sandy had said, since without any water his ears weren't working properly, but he wasn't about to turn back now.

Without the bulky diving suit, Sandy looked quite different. She had brown fur and was dressed in a pink polka-dot bikini top and skirt.

"Yup, that's how I like my air," SpongeBob said, taking in a deep breath. "Dry as dirt . . . with no water!"

"All right!" Sandy cheered, doing a cartwheel. "I made Texas Tea and El Paso Grande Hot Spicy Cookies! Come on in, I'll give ya the grand tour!"

She skipped across the grass, expecting SpongeBob to follow.

But SpongeBob couldn't move. His legs were like baked clay, and locked in place.

Sandy glanced back over her shoulder. SpongeBob still had the same creepy smile, only more of his teeth were now showing as the skin on his face continued to tighten in the hot sun.

"You sure are a funny little dude," Sandy

snorted as she hopped behind SpongeBob and pushed him toward the picnic table under her giant oak tree.

"Thank you," SpongeBob replied as they sat down at the table. As his knees bent, they made loud popping noises, like firecrackers.

"So, this is my own private little air bubble," Sandy said, chattering away. "This air is the driest, purest, most airiest air in the whole dang sea!"

SpongeBob gasped in agreement.

Sandy pointed to a birdbath made of stone. "Over there is my birdbath."

Inside the birdbath, an orange bird played happily in the water.

Water!

Never had that word sounded so beautiful to SpongeBob.

Sandy babbled on, paying no mind to her guest's distress. "That's my oak tree!" she said, pointing up. "It provides me with extra air!"

SpongeBob nodded once as he focused on the birdbath.

The bird chirped happily, splashing as it bathed, throwing away precious glistening drops of cool, wet water.

"This dome is made of polyurethane. That's a fancy name for plastic," Sandy continued. "Ain't that the bees knees?"

SpongeBob wheezed in agreement, waiting for his chance. He had to get into that birdbath . . . before it was too late!

chapter six

The time for SpongeBob to make his move came when Sandy got up to check on her cookies in the kitchen.

In a blur of speed, he leaped across the grass and sprang into the air, landing on his face in the center of the birdbath!

Each and every inch of SpongeBob's body soaked up the precious water, leaving nothing but one angry chattering bird!

Then, like lightning, SpongeBob flew back to

his position across from the returning Sandy, who never knew he had left!

"Do you like my home?" she asked.

"It's very nice," SpongeBob said, sounding like an old, old man as his throat whined for more water. What he had absorbed from the birdbath had been refreshing, but it was not enough.

SpongeBob needed *more* water.

"Over there's my treadmill," Sandy said, pointing to her exercise equipment. "That's how I stay in tip-top shape."

"Water?" SpongeBob said in a faint wisp of a voice.

"You want something to drink? Glad to oblige! Let's have that tea now!" Sandy said, opening the door in the base of the oak tree. "I'll run down and grab us a pitcher!"

After Sandy left for the tea, SpongeBob heard a knocking sound.

He turned and spotted Patrick outside the

dome. Patrick, who was standing in the blue-green waters of the ocean.

"Flowers!" Patrick yelled, but SpongeBob could barely hear him through the thick polyurethane of Sandy's treedome.

The starfish mimed holding up the bouquet of sea flowers.

SpongeBob looked down. His sea flowers were wilting without water.

Kind of like SpongeBob himself.

"Come and get it!" Sandy announced, bringing up the iced tea.

"I brought you some flowers," SpongeBob gasped.

"For little ol' me? How sweet!" Sandy replied, reaching over to take the gift.

SpongeBob's fingers were locked in place, dried like twigs around the stems of the flower arrangement.

"Umph!" Sandy said, tugging away.

SNAP!

Two of SpongeBob's fingers broke as Sandy retrieved the flowers.

Sandy looked down at the fingers and peered closely at SpongeBob. The little yellow sponge was in sad shape. The water from the birdbath was long gone.

"You okay?" a concerned Sandy asked.

"Yyyyesss, I'm okay," SpongeBob replied, his raspy voice now sounding like an old straw broom sweeping across a wooden kitchen floor.

Sandy wasn't so sure, but she didn't want to embarrass her guest. "You know," she said, trying to change the subject, "you're the first sea critter to ever visit!"

"I can't imagine why," SpongeBob said, coughing.

"Me neither," Sandy said, standing up with the flowers. "I'm gonna put these in a vase."

"Take your time," SpongeBob said.

The instant she was gone, SpongeBob lunged for the treedome exit, but his legs were as stiff as dried leather. He could no longer bend his knees.

I've got to get out of here, SpongeBob thought.

Too hot.

Too dry.

"Must . . . escape . . . treedome," SpongeBob whispered. "Must escape . . . *now!*"

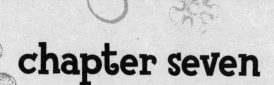

chapter seven

SpongeBob imagined himself turning the knob to the heavy steel door and plunging into wonderful, slippery seawater.

Just then, Sandy reappeared, holding a clear glass vase filled with the sea flowers. "Why, these flowers are just beautiful," the squirrel said as she sat the vase down on the picnic table. "And they'll live *much* longer in a vase of ice . . . cold . . . water."

I don't need it. I don't need it, SpongeBob thought

to himself, repeating the phrase over and over . . . staring at the vase of flowers in front of him.

A vase filled with water and cubes of ice! Ice water!

SpongeBob felt like crying, but he was so dried out, he had no tears left.

"So, tell me about yourself. It must be fascinating being a sea critter!" Sandy said brightly, trying to make conversation.

"Some days are better than others," SpongeBob rasped.

"I can't imagine growing up under the ocean. I grew up in wide-open spaces, where I could run and jump in the sun . . . ," Sandy continued dreamily, letting her voice trail off.

"SpongeBob?" she asked, waving a paw in front of his slack-jawed face.

DING!

A bell went off from inside Sandy's kitchen.

"Oh! There's the cookies!" she announced,

running back to the tree. "Be right back."

"I don't need it! I don't need it!" SpongeBob whispered over and over again. Before him sat the vase. Beads of liquid condensation slid down one side of the glass, pooling at the bottom on the table.

Silence.

"I . . . I . . . I . . . NEEEEEEED IT!" SpongeBob screamed, blasting off like a rocket into the hot Texas air. He shot straight up into the sky, bounced off the roof of the treedome, and landed in a crouch next to the vase of water.

Wheezing in triumph, he snatched the container and threw away the flowers! Picking up the vase in both hands, he was ready to guzzle!

KNOCK! KNOCK! KNOCK!

SpongeBob ignored the sounds. He knew that Patrick was watching this breach of social etiquette with an expression of sheer horror.

"Nooooooooooooooo!" the starfish yelled as he

jumped up and down outside of the dome.

SpongeBob managed to turn his dry, brittle neck and look at his friend.

"No, SpongeBob! No! Stop! Pinkie out! Pinkie!" Patrick cried in a faint voice that was muffled by the thick plastic of the protective dome.

SpongeBob didn't care. He greedily gulped down the soothing ice water!

But the puny vase full of water was not enough to quench his need for water! He was a sponge! Sponges need water, and lots of it! Everybody knew that! Air, phooey! Bring on the liquid refreshment!

SpongeBob ran to the exit . . . only to find the way out blocked by his best friend!

"Where do you think you're going?" Patrick asked.

chapter eight

Slamming the steel door shut, Patrick picked SpongeBob up from the grass. "What's wrong, lil' buddy?" he asked.

"I'm a quitter!" SpongeBob sobbed. "Waaaaah!"

Patrick frowned. "You can't leave now, SpongeBob! You'll blow it!" he said.

"Air is not good, Patrick," he said in a defeated tone. "Air is *not* good."

Patrick tucked SpongeBob under one arm like an overdue library book and began the long walk back to the picnic table. "You're just being shy," he said cheerfully. "Don't worry! You're doing fine!

"Nope, not gonna let you blow this," Patrick continued. He gulped. Sandy's picnic table seemed a million miles away. Patrick tried to swallow, but his throat was as dry as a piece of coral.

"Sure is hot in here," the starfish said, dropping SpongeBob and flopping down on the ground. The two friends looked at each other.

"Gosh, SpongeBob," Patrick said, realizing his friend's problem for the very first time. "You don't look so good."

Patrick gasped, but not at SpongeBob's appearance. Suddenly he discovered it was getting very hard to breathe.

His vision was blurring, too. And when he wiped his brow, Patrick discovered his skin felt like it was made of sandpaper! "What kind of place is this?!?" the starfish bellowed.

"T-tr-treedome," SpongeBob answered slowly. "Full of . . . *air.*"

"You mean there's no *water* in here?" Patrick cried, crawling on his hands and knees toward the exit. "We've gotta get outta here!"

"I tried to tell you," SpongeBob said as he crawled after Patrick. "You wouldn't listen."

"I'm listening now!" Patrick yelled. He got to his feet and pounded on the steel door that led out of the treedome. "Let us out! We need water!"

Together Patrick and SpongeBob tried to open the door, but in their weakened condition, they couldn't budge it. Both friends slid to the grass, slumped in defeat.

"Looks like this is the end, old chum," SpongeBob said.

"Next time you get invited to a tea party . . . ," Patrick replied, his voice trailing off.

"Yes?" SpongeBob asked.

Patrick licked his dry lips. "Count me out."

chapter nine

SpongeBob SquarePants was having the most pleasant dream.

He was at a swanky beach party at Goo Lagoon, and all of his friends were there.

Patrick was doing the limbo under a seaweed string, and Mr. Krabs was busy cooking up a grill full of Krabby Patties. SpongeBob's new pal Sandy was lifting weights and impressing everyone with her astonishing strength.

His pet snail, Gary, was off to one side mewing

happily as SpongeBob gave him a pat on the head. Even grumpy old Squidward appeared to be enjoying himself as he played a jazzy tune on his clarinet.

And best of all, there was water everywhere.

He gave a long sigh of relief. Water splashed to his left, and flowed to his right.

SpongeBob opened his eyes. A familiar blue-green haze hung in front of his vision like a curtain.

He smacked his lips. Something tasted wet!

Could it be . . . ? Yes, it was water! Sweet, sweet water!

"Rise and shine, SpongeBob," Sandy said. "Y'all gave me quite the scare! You two were dried up like beef jerky on a North Dallas blacktop!"

SpongeBob looked up and saw Sandy was standing on a ladder. She was holding a garden hose. A steady stream of water was pouring out of the hose and into the open tops of the glass

helmets that SpongeBob and Patrick were now wearing.

"I modified some of my old air helmets," Sandy said. "Turns out they hold water just as good as air!"

SpongeBob stood up and stretched as Sandy finished filling his helmet.

"There, that oughta do it," she said, turning off the hose. "How do you feel?"

"Like a brand-new sponge!" SpongeBob replied.

"Me too!" Patrick added. "Well, maybe not like a sponge, but I feel brand-new."

SpongeBob looked down at the tops of his sensible black shoes. He couldn't look Sandy in the eye. "I'm sorry for all the trouble," he said.

The squirrel laughed. "Weren't no trouble. If ya'll needed water . . . you shoulda asked!"

"Yeah, SpongeBob," Patrick said. "You should have asked."

SpongeBob glared Patrick. "As I recall," he said in a frosty tone, "someone taught me asking for stuff at a tea party was bad manners."

"Really?" Patrick said innocently. "Who was that?"

Stepping off the ladder, Sandy fetched a tray with three glasses of home-brewed Texas Iced Tea and a platter of cookies. "Well, now that you're back to normal, let's have our goodies," she said.

Everyone took a glass of tea.

"I propose a toast," Sandy announced, holding out her glass. "To new friends!"

"To new friends," SpongeBob and Patrick agreed, tilting their glasses for a drink . . . and spilling the tea down the fronts of their water helmets.

"Hold on a second," Sandy said. "I got an idea."

She climbed back up the ladder and dropped a tea bag into SpongeBob's and Patrick's helmets.

Inside the glass containers the water started to change color from pale blue into a lovely golden shade of brown.

"Drink up!" Sandy announced.

"Ahem." Patrick cleared his throat. He then held up his pinkie.

SpongeBob giggled and held up his pinkie too.

Sandy shrugged. She was still getting used to the strange ways of these sea critters. She also stuck out her pinkie.

Everyone took a long, cool drink of their tea and smiled.

"Ahhhhh!" SpongeBob said. "Delicious!"

about the author

Terry Collins has written hundreds of stories for children, many of them featuring characters from Nickelodeon such as *CatDog, Ren and Stimpy,* and now *SpongeBob SquarePants*! A former newspaper reporter and columnist, he's also active in theater arts and teaches acting when not chained to the typewriter. A lifelong lover of books, Terry is glad he doesn't live under the sea since the saltwater tends to make the pages soggy. Instead, he makes the mountains of North Carolina his home, with his wife, Ginny, and their four dogs, Chico, Jaws, Sweetie, and Josie.